Y0-EDX-124

A Note to Parents and Caregivers:

With a focus on math, science, and social studies, *Read-it!* Readers support both the learning of content information and the extension of more complex reading skills. They encourage the development of problem-solving skills that help children expand their thinking.

 The PURPLE LEVEL presents basic topics and objects using high frequency words and simple language patterns.

 The RED LEVEL presents familiar topics using common words and repeating sentence patterns.

 The BLUE LEVEL presents new ideas using a larger vocabulary and varied sentence structure.

 The YELLOW LEVEL presents more challenging ideas, a broad vocabulary, and wide variety in sentence structure.

 The GREEN LEVEL presents more complex ideas, an extended vocabulary range, and expanded language structures.

 The ORANGE LEVEL presents a wide range of ideas and concepts using challenging vocabulary and complex language structures.

When sharing a content focused book with your child, read to find out facts and concepts, pausing often to restate and talk about the new information. The realistic story format provides an opportunity to talk about the language used, and to learn about reading to problem-solve for information. Encourage children to measure, make maps, and consider other situations that allow them to apply what they are learning.

There is no right or wrong way to share books with children. Find time to read and share new learning with your child, and pass on the legacy of literacy.

Adria F. Klein, Ph.D.
Professor Emeritus
California State University
San Bernardino, California

Editor: Jill Kalz
Designer: Tracy Davies
Page Production: Melissa Kes
Art Director: Nathan Gassman
Associate Managing Editor: Christianne Jones
The illustrations in this book were created with mixed media.

Picture Window Books
151 Good Counsel Drive
P.O. Box 669
Mankato, MN 56002-0669
877-845-8392
www.picturewindowbooks.com

Printed in the United States of America.

All books published by Picture Window Books
are manufactured with paper containing at least
10 percent post-consumer waste.

Library of Congress Cataloging-in-Publication Data
Shaskan, Trisha Speed, 1973-
Green Park / by Trisha Speed Shaskan ; illustrated by Esther Loopstra.
p. cm. — (Read-it! readers: character education)
ISBN 978-1-4048-4232-8 (library binding)
ISBN 978-1-4048-4236-6 (paperback)
1. Citizenship—Juvenile literature. I. Loopstra, Esther Dawn, 1976- ill.
II. Title.
JF801.S46 2009
323.6—dc22   2008007169

BY TRISHA SPEED SHASKAN
ILLUSTRATED BY ESTHER LOOPSTRA

Special thanks to our advisers for their expertise:

Kay A. Augustine, ED.S.
National Character Development Trainer and Consultant

Adria F. Klein, Ph.D.
Professor Emeritus, California State University
San Bernardino, California

PICTURE WINDOW BOOKS
Minneapolis, Minnesota

Jade, Olive, and Kelly were best friends. They lived near each other.

They played together at Green Park.

4

Jade liked to paint. She painted pictures of her friends.

At Green Park, Jade drew on the sidewalks with colorful chalk.

Olive liked to garden. In the spring, she helped her parents plant flowers and vegetables.

At Green Park, Olive dug in the dirt.

Kelly liked to build things. She helped her dad build benches.

At Green Park, Kelly built things out of twigs.

One summer day, Jade, Olive, and Kelly were sitting under a tree at Green Park. The park director, Mrs. Moss, saw them and waved. "Hi, kids," she said. "Next week is Citizenship Week! We need to come up with a project."

"What is citizenship?" asked Kelly.

"Citizenship means doing whatever you can to make the place where you live better," said Mrs. Moss. "It means being a good neighbor. It means showing your community that you care."

"We're going to pick one project to do at Green Park," Mrs. Moss said.

"Only one project?" asked Kelly.

"One project that we can all work on together," Mrs. Moss said. "For example, we could pick up trash. Or we could have a community concert. You three think about it, and I'll be back later."

Jade looked around. She saw a candy bar wrapper. "We could paint signs that tell people not to litter," she said.

"I can't paint as well as you can," said Kelly.

"Me, neither," said Olive.

Jade drew a sad face on the sidewalk.

11

Olive looked around. She saw trees and grass. But she didn't see any flowers. "We could plant flowers," she said.

"I don't know much about gardening," said Jade.

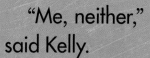

"Me, neither," said Kelly.

Olive looked at the dirt and frowned.

Kelly looked around. She saw only a few places for people to sit. "We could build a bench or two," she said.

"That's not as much fun as painting signs," said Jade.

"Or planting flowers," said Olive.
"I think it would be fun," said Kelly. She looked at the twigs in her hands and frowned.

15

Jade, Olive, and Kelly sat in silence. Soon Mrs. Moss came back.

"Do you have any ideas?" she asked.

"I wanted to paint signs to tell people not to litter," said Jade. "But no one else wanted to."

"I wanted to plant flowers," said Olive. "But no one else wanted to."

"I wanted to build a bench or two," said Kelly. "But no one else wanted to."

"I like the sign idea," said Mrs. Moss. "Flowers would make the park pretty. And there aren't enough benches here. You all have good ideas."

"Some are better than others," said Kelly.

"No, they aren't," said Jade.

Olive just looked at the dirt.

"Girls," said Mrs. Moss, "citizenship means coming together for the community. It means working together. Once you agree on one project, come talk to me."

After Mrs. Moss left, Jade drew a flower on the sidewalk. It gave Olive an idea.

"Jade," she said, "you could make signs that ask people to help us plant flowers."

"Sounds good," Jade said.

"My dad would help us build a bench by the flowers," Kelly said.

"I'm sure my parents would help plant the flowers," said Olive.

Jade, Olive, and Kelly walked into the park office. Mrs. Moss was at her desk.

"We thought of an idea," said Jade. "We're going to plant a flower garden."

"We're going to make a bench for the garden, too," said Kelly.

"Great," said Mrs. Moss. "Now you're working together."

The next day, Jade and a couple other kids started painting and hanging signs.

Mrs. Moss took Olive to the store to buy flowers. They bought vegetable seeds, too.

Kelly and her dad went to the hardware store.
They bought wood and screws for the bench.

Saturday morning, the sun shined brightly on Green Park. Jade, Olive, and Kelly came to the park with their families. Mrs. Moss was already waiting there.

"Mrs. Moss, what if no one comes?" Olive asked. "We can't do everything by ourselves." "Don't worry," Mrs. Moss said. "You'll see."

Soon a big group of parents, grandparents, and kids showed up. They carried shovels, hoes, and other tools. They were ready to work.

"I've never seen this many people at the park," said Jade.

"Or this many gardening tools," said Olive.

"We saw the signs,"
said one of the women.

"We wanted to help out,"
said one of the men.

"What a great neighborhood we have,"
said Mrs. Moss.

29

Before long, Green Park Community Garden started to grow. Everyone took turns watering the plants. They took turns pulling weeds. Jade, Olive, and Kelly were proud of the garden.

"And we all did it together!" said Mrs. Moss.

Citizenship Day Activity

Have a Citizenship Day! Gather a few friends and decide what you can do for your community.

Here are some ideas:
- Start a neighborhood clean-up day. Pick up trash found on the sidewalks, grass, in the park, or your backyard.
- Help elderly people. Offer to rake or clean up the yards of the elderly people who live near you or your school.
- With the help of a grown-up, plant a garden at school or at the park near your house.
- On a cold day, gather a group of friends and shovel the sidewalks.

Remember that citizenship means coming together for the good of your community. The activity you do can be as simple as picking up trash or as big as planting a community garden. The important thing is that you work together with the people in your community to make it a better place.

Glossary

citizen—a member of a community, such as a town or country

citizenship—the duties that come with being a member of a community

community—a group of people who live in the same area

To Learn More

More Books to Read

Kishel, Ann-Marie. *Citizenship*. Minneapolis: Lerner Publications
    Company, 2007.
Riehecky, Janet. *Citizenship*. Mankato, Minn.: Capstone Press, 2005.
Small, Mary. *Being a Good Citizen*. Minneapolis: Picture Window
    Books, 2006.

On the Web

FactHound offers a safe, fun way to find Web sites related to topics
in this book. All of the sites on FactHound have been researched
by our staff.

1. Visit www.facthound.com
2. Type in this special code:
   1404842322
3. Click on the FETCH IT button.

Your trusty FactHound will fetch the best sites for you!

Look for books in the *Read-it!* Readers: Character Education series:

Fair Game (character education: fairness)
Green Park (character education: citizenship)